WEDNESDAY THURSDAY

SUNDAY

by Beatrice Schenk de Regniers

What Did You Put in Your Pocket?

illustrated by Michael Grejniec

HarperCollins Publishers

What Did You Put in Your Pocket?

Text copyright © 1958, 1986 by Beatrice Schenk de Regniers
Illustrations copyright © 2003 by Michael Grejniec
Manufactured in China.   All rights reserved.
www.harperchildrens.com

Library of Congress Cataloging-in-Publication Data
De Regniers, Beatrice Schenk.
What did you put in your pocket? / by Beatrice
Schenk de Regniers ; pictures by Michael Grejniec.
          p.   cm.
Summary: Two groups of animals tell each other about
the food and other things that they put in their pockets.
ISBN 0-06-029028-5 —— ISBN 0-06-029029-3 (lib.bdg.)
[1. Pockets—Fiction. 2. Days—Fiction. 3. Food—Fiction.
4. Animals—Fiction.] I. Grejniec, Michael, ill. II. Title.
PZ7.D4417 Wi 2003   2002022873
                                                [E]—dc21
Typography by Ayako Hosono and Michael Grejniec
                    1 2 3 4 5 6 7 8 9 10
                                              ❖
                              First Edition

For Carol Minami

— B. S. d R.

For the man who mistook his wife for a hat

— M. G.

What did
you put
in your pocket

what did you put
in your pocket

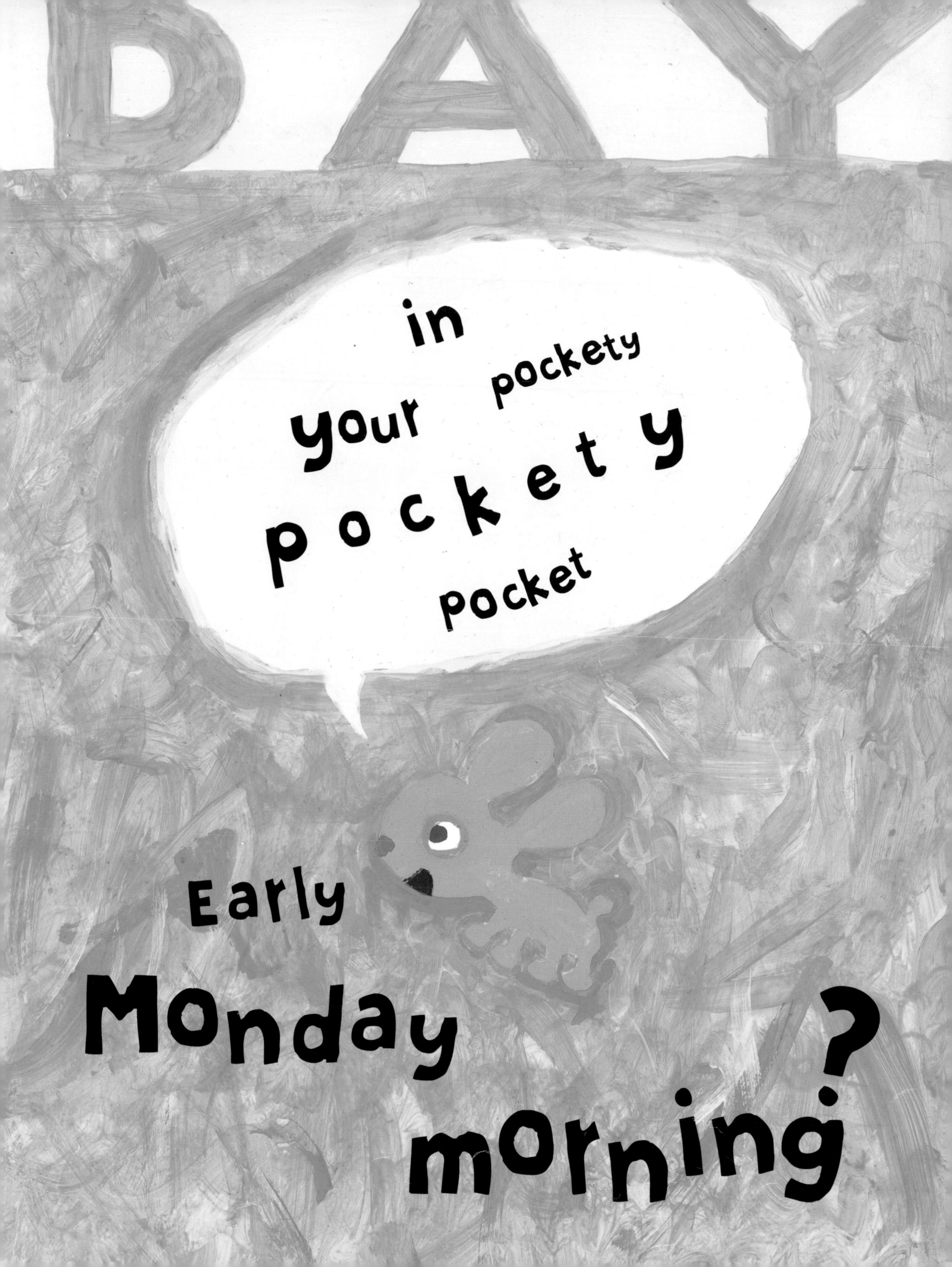

in
your pockety
p o c k e t y
pocket

Early
Monday
morning?

I put in some chocolate pudding

I put in some chocolate pudding

slushy glushy pudding

Early Monday morning.

I put in some ice-cold water

I put in some ice-cold water

nicy icy water

Early Tuesday morning.

I put in a scoop of ice cream

I put in a scoop of ice cream

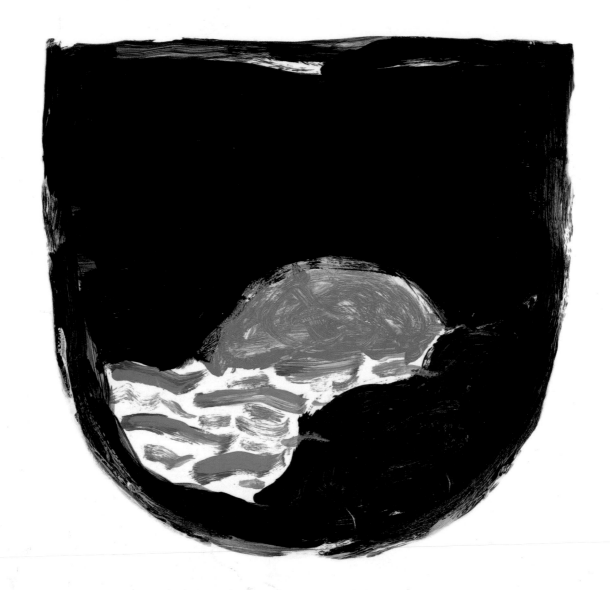

slurpy glurpy ice cream

Early Wednesday morning.

Slushy glushy
Pudding!

Nicy icy
water!

Slurpy glurpy
ice cream!

I put in some mashed potatoes

I put in some mashed potatoes

fluppy gluppy potatoes

Early Thursday morning.

Slushy glushy
pudding!

Nicy icy
water!!

Slurpy glurpy
ice cream!

Fluppy gluppy
potatoes!!

in
What did you
put
in
your
pocket
p o c k e
p
What did you
put in your
pocket

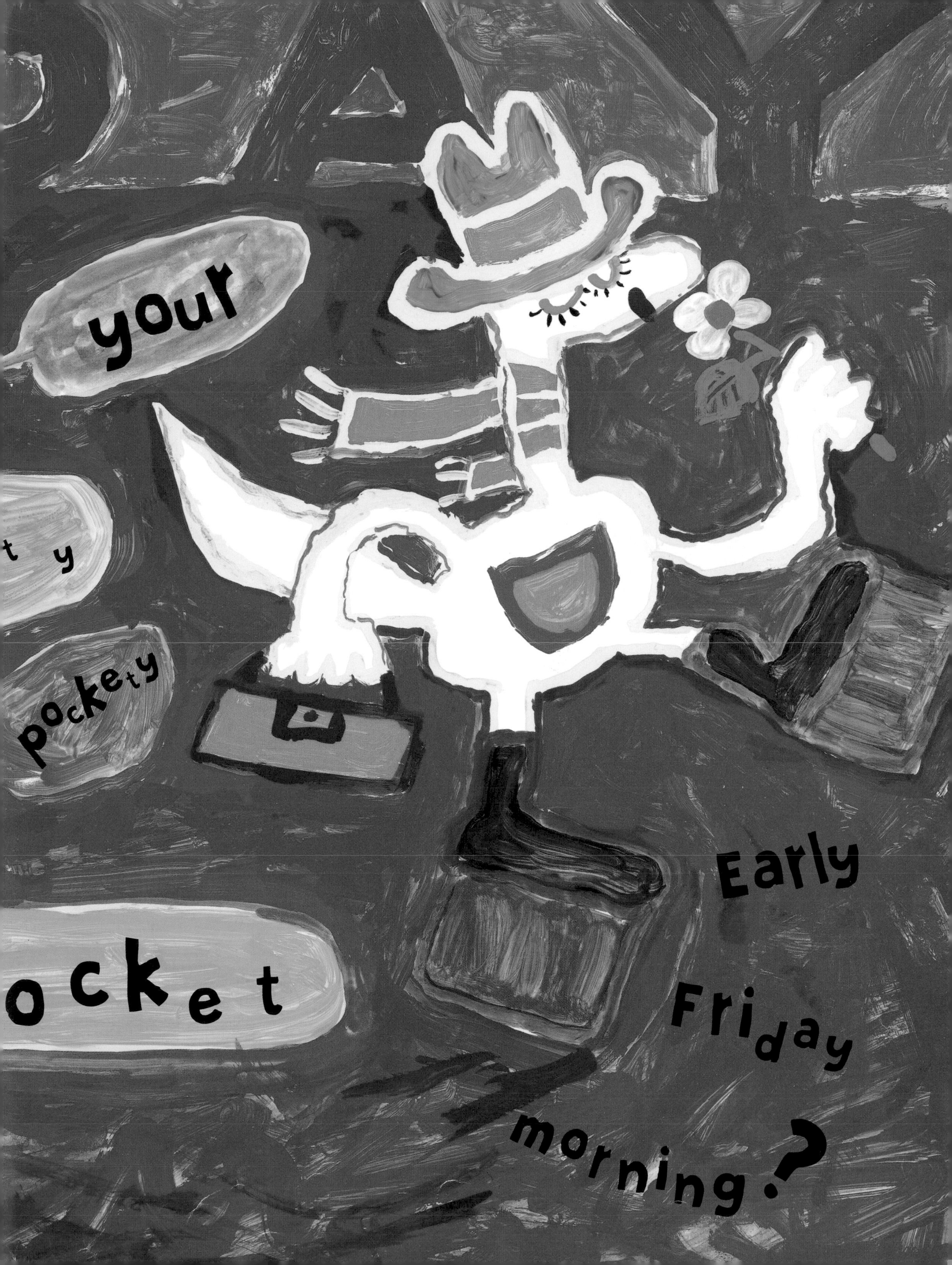
your
t y
pockety
ocket
Early Friday morning?

I put in some sticky molasses

I put in some sticky molasses

sticky icky molasses

Early Friday morning.

Slushy glushy pudaing!

Nicy icy water!

Slurpy gluppy ice cream!

Fluppy gluppy potatoes!

Sticky icky molasses!

I put in my five fingers

I put in my five fingers

funny finny fingers

Early Saturday morning.

Slushy glushy pudding!

Nicy icy water!

Slurpy glurpy ice cream!

Fluppy gluppy potatoes!

Sticky icky molasses!

Funny finny fingers!

SUN
What did you put
in your pocket
What did you put
in
your
pocket
in
your
pockety

I put in a clean white handkerchief

I put in a clean white handkerchief

a spinky spanky handkerchief

Early Sunday morning.

Slushy glushy pudding!

Nicy icy water!!

Slurpy glurpy ice cream!

Fluppy gluppy potatoas!

Sticky icky molasses!

Funny finny fingers!

Spinky spanky handkerchief!

MONDAY TUESDAY

FRIDAY SATURDAY